Acting Edition

Spain

by Jen Silverman

ISBN 978-0-573-71110-7

www.concordtheatricals.com
www.concordtheatricals.co.uk

FOR PRODUCTION INQUIRIES

UNITED STATES AND CANADA
info@concordtheatricals.com
1-866-979-0447

UNITED KINGDOM AND EUROPE
licensing@concordtheatricals.co.uk
020-7054-7298

This work is published by Samuel French, an imprint of Concord Theatricals Corp.

SPAIN was commissioned by and premiered at Second Stage Theater (Carole Rothman, President and Artistic Director; Lisa Lawer Post, Executive Director) in October 2023. It was directed by Tyne Rafaeli, with scenic design by Dane Laffrey, costume design by Alejo Vietti, lighting design by Jen Schriever, original music and sound design by Daniel Kluger, and props by Ray Wetmore. The production stage manager was Lisa Chernoff and the stage manager was Kaitlin Marsh. The cast was as follows:

JORIS.. Andrew Burnap
HELEN.. Marin Ireland
DOS.. Erik Lochtefeld
ERNEST.. Danny Wolohan
KARL................................ Zachary James and Tom Nelis

The production was supported by a generous enhancement from MacPac Entertainment LLC and was the recipient of the Blanche and Irving Laurie Foundation Theatre Visions Fund Award.

CHARACTERS

JORIS IVENS – man, 30s, wants to be liked, easygoing, an infiltrator

HELEN – woman, 30s, sharp, pragmatic, an infiltrator

JOHN DOS PASSOS (DOS) – man, early 40s, a deeply decent man who can be naïve

ERNEST HEMINGWAY – man, late 30s, charming, secretly self-hating, overcompensates

KARL – man, can be 40s–60s, should speak Russian, also plays **IVOR**

SETTING

The West Village. Sort of.

In the stage directions, I describe a giant, soaring back wall into which are built secret panels and windows. The wall serves as a delivery device for characters, moments, world-size shifts. Other designs are possible and encouraged. In fact, in *Spain*'s world premiere, though we built a wall, we facilitated a number of the sudden reveals via a turntable and focused lighting instead of wall panels.

What is crucial for your set is a sense of intimidating mystery, an unchanging façade of some kind – and its ability to shift into sudden and surprising revelations.

TIME

1936...ish

AUTHOR'S NOTES

(Words in parentheses) are an aside or a sub-thought.

Words in bold are spoken into a microphone.

The spacing is a gesture toward indicating rhythm: how thoughts change, escalate, or get supplanted by other thoughts as we talk. The line breaks often signal shifts, but do *not* indicate a beat or pause except where written.

This is not
A history play.

This wants to feel
Anachronistic. Shape-shifting. Contemporary.

A note on historical context

In 1936, the Dutch filmmaker Joris Ivens was hired to make a movie about the Spanish Civil War, which was underway. Though Joris was the front-man, there is some proof that the movie was conceived and engineered by Soviet agents of the propaganda bureau.

The revolutionary Spanish government was full of high-level Soviet military pulling the strings, and they intended for Joris to create a piece of skillful, visceral propaganda that would garner American sympathies, undo Roosevelt's non-intervention policy, and direct American donations to the Spanish communists. Joris and his girlfriend were deeply and knowingly embedded in this Soviet machine. The American writers that Joris hired were not.

The context above provided the seeds from which this theatrical fiction was built. But most crucially, *Spain* is not about history – it is in a sideways, theatrical conversation with the contemporary moment, in which we too are navigating questions of art and power and disinformation.

One

(A West Village apartment from 1936.)

*(***JORIS*** talks to us. Conversational but urgent.)*

(We are going to help him make the biggest decision of his life.)

JORIS. The way it happened was

the KGB called me in

(they weren't calling themselves that, obviously, it was

the Office of the Branch of International Cultural Socialist Whatever Whatever

but – the KGB)

and they said: Make A Movie About Spain.

I said: I've never been to Spain.

And they said: You Don't Have To Have Been To Spain

To Understand What Spain Is.

(Genuinely wondering.)

Is that true?

(Hmm, well, what is *Spain:)*

I'm thinking...uh...tapas. And...bull fighting. And...

Don Quixote!

And...

Rioja! Right?

Tempranillo?

But anyway, the basics, I just think of the basics.

We're having this conversation at an expensive hotel

on the East Side, far away from the Village

so that nobody I know would see me and wonder who I'm talking to

and we order the steak

(I get mine well done, he gets his rare)

and then my handler –

ugh, I don't like that word, "handler"

let's say my *dinner companion* –

my Dinner Companion says:

Joris.

Joris, As You Know, There Is A Civil War In Spain

And War Can Get So Complicated If You Try To Understand All The Different Bits

Who Did What To Whom –

But Your Movie Will Keep It Simple!

The War In Spain Is A War

Between The Rich And The Poor

The Noble Peasant Crushed by The Rich Fascist

See?

A Single-Sentence War

And a Single-Sentence War is a Perfect Opportunity for...

– and then he said: ART

but we both knew that wasn't the word he meant.

(A spotlight comes up on the wall behind **JORIS.***)*

(A panel opens to reveal: a **MAN** *seated at a table, cutting and eating bloody steak. We can't see his face. We might not even be able to see his entire body. Our vision should be focused – whether via the architecture of the set, or the lights – on that bloody steak.)*

(This is Joris's handler, **KARL.***)*

(He rhythmically cuts and eats steak all through the following:)

He said:

Joris, This Movie Is About

How Hard It Is For A Farmer To Till The Blood-Drenched Soil.

He said:

It Must Be Very Moving, Visceral and Moving

Americans Should Feel Sadness And Pity And Sympathy

And The Desire to Send Money

(Despite This Whole Non-Intervention Thing.)

He said:

But You Can't Mention Russians.

No Russians.

Nobody Can Even Think About Russians.

If There Are Russians In Spain, They're Just Visiting.

They're Entirely Uninvolved In Governmental Decisions

And They Have Nothing To Do With The War.

Write About Spain. As Metaphor.

And then he said: Let's Make This Movie Long.

*(**KARL** vanishes. **JORIS** is alone again.)*

I'm a filmmaker. What can I say? I *love* metaphors.

And I love the working-class

(in theory, obviously)

and look, I've been working with Russians for a long time

this particular branch of Russians,

and yes, they sort of specialize in middle of the night secret assassinations but

they've funded a *lot* of my films, which –

you know, financing is complicated

when it comes to the arts –

So when he said *Make This Movie Long...*

(Genuinely excited, film-nerd side emerging.)

Like, who gets to make anything *long*?

My last film? Fifteen minutes.

The one before that? Ten.

How long is *Long*? You know? Like...forty minutes?

(A beat.)

But, like I said, I've never been to Spain.

I need to be honest about that. So I said:

Maybe there's a Spanish guy who might, you know, be better for this?

And my ha–

(Catches himself as he starts to say "handler.")

dinner companion

looked me in the eyes and said:

(We reveal **KARL** *again. As before, we do not see him fully – perhaps a panel opens and we see only his hands. Or* **KARL** *appears, but his face and body are in shadow.)*

(Either way **KARL***'s hands are pouring wine. The glass seems to be bottomless because he's just pouring and pouring and pouring wine through the following:)*

We Don't Need A Spanish Guy.

They'd Add Too Many Details

Or The Wrong Details.

We Need You.

Make A Movie, Joris.

*(***KARL*** vanishes.)*

(Oh, **JORIS** *forgot to clarify:)*

That's me: Joris. I'm Joris.

I'm Dutch, and I'm talking to you with a light Dutch accent –

(He isn't, he speaks with an accent standard to wherever this play is being done.)

– and as I've said, I make documentary films. I live for my art. And though my recent work has been, uh, a collaboration by necessity with the KGB – someday, I'll make work that's mine alone again.

But today it's 1936, and I'm in a hotel on the East Side

in which there are at least five special agents

lurking in five different suites

who could hunt me down and assassinate me at any moment –

so I consider my dinner companion's proposition

for about as long as he might expect me to pretend to consider it

but it's not like there's too much to think about.

And we both know it.

(**JORIS** *shrugs.)*

Spain!

What's not to love about Spain?

Two

(**HELEN** *enters. She's his girlfriend.)*

(Also works for the KGB. Also a filmmaker.)

(They were sort of assigned to each other, but also, there's real chemistry even when they're arguing.)

(Mid-conversation.)

HELEN. – But we've never *been* to Spain.

JORIS. No I know...

HELEN. I mean, I don't even know what they –

JORIS. Spanish. They speak Spanish.

HELEN. I *know* they speak Spanish

oh my god

I was gonna say, I don't even know what they're *like.*

JORIS. *(Shrugs.)* People are people everywhere.

HELEN. Is that the thesis for our little movie?

"People are people everywhere"?

JORIS. Uh, no Helen, the thesis is: The Working Man Tills The Blood-Drenched Soil.

(**HELEN** *finds she actually likes this.)*

HELEN. Oh, that's nice.

JORIS. *(Surprised, then pleased.)* You think?

HELEN. Yeah. We could do a lot with that.

JORIS. *(Coaxing.)* I'm noticing the "we."

HELEN. You know I'm a filmmaker too.

I'm not just your assigned girlfriend.

JORIS. *(Re: "assigned.")* Careful with that.

I never said you were *just* anything.

HELEN. Next time you have dinner with Karl, remind him that I'm a filmmaker too.

(This makes **JORIS** *very nervous. Lowering his voice –)*

JORIS. We're not supposed to say his name.

HELEN. Oh come on, you know it's not his real name.

JORIS. Even so. My Dinner Companion –

HELEN. Karl.

JORIS. My Dinner Companion –

HELEN. Karl.

JORIS. Helen!!

HELEN. You think he's gonna pop out of the chimney?

JORIS. Helen, I'm telling you.

HELEN. That's probably not even *my* name.

(A surprised and fragile silence between them.)

*(***JORIS** *is stung. She's opened a can of worms she shouldn't.)*

...Kidding!

*(***JORIS** *is silent.)*

Don't look like that.

I was kidding.

Joris.

Come on.

You *know* my name is Helen.

JORIS. *(A little stiffly.)* I only know what you tell me, Helen.

HELEN. OK are we doing this again? Let's not do this.

JORIS. Do what? You started it.

HELEN. Well I'm sorry I ever brought up K–

your *Dinner Companion.*

You know my name is Helen.

JORIS. Frankly, it shouldn't matter, should it. What's in a name.

Shouldn't matter what we go by if we want the same things.

HELEN. Your name might not even be Joris.

JORIS. ...My name *is* Joris.

It's not the kind of name you make up.

HELEN. No I know.

JORIS. *(Back to work.)* Anyway, Our Dinner Companion said we have to fast-track this.

HELEN. ...Also I vetted you, so I know.

*(**JORIS** is knocked off-balance again.)*

JORIS. You *vetted* me?

HELEN. When Karl – sorry! (Sorry. But he said I could call him Karl, so I'm just gonna call him Karl because I feel like a fucking idiot calling him Your Dinner Companion so)

ANYWAY

when Karl introduced you to me as a concept

(before he introduced you to me as a person)

We were having dinner

and he said: There's This Filmmaker I Would Like You To Meet

Who Is Going To Be Very Important To The Movement

His Name is Joris Ivens.

And I said, Sure, Karl.

And then I left that hotel and I walked fifteen blocks north and three blocks west

to a different hotel

where I checked in under a different name

and made a call to a different guy, let's call him Ivor –

(A door in the wall opens to reveal: a shadowy **MAN**. *We can't see his face. We might not even be able to see his entire body. He clips the end off a thick cigar: Shhk! He lights the cigar and smokes.)*

– and I asked Ivor about you. *And* about Karl.

He said Karl is an asshole, and obsessed with opera, and maybe gay?

and technically his subordinate, although they're in different branches of the same branch,

and Karl can't know he exists,

and I should never say the name Ivor to anyone,

and then he said that you were really named Joris.

And that everyone liked you.

*(***IVOR***'s door shuts with a thunk.)*

(A beat between them. So much about this is shocking that **JORIS** *defaults to the nearest, least consequential question:)*

JORIS. (He said everyone likes me?)

HELEN. (Yeah.)

(This is a pleasant surprise.)

JORIS. (Oh.)

HELEN. (You're the life of the party, you know that you're liked, it's your secret weapon.)

JORIS. (No, I know but)

HELEN. (You're likable, you're deployed to be likable

I'm hot, I'm deployed to be hot

– I guess I also have to be likable

but it's different / for –)

*(**JORIS** has regained himself enough to ask the largest and most combustible question. He cuts in:)*

JORIS. "Let's call him Ivor" or "His name is Ivor"?

HELEN. ...What?

JORIS. You said: "Let's call him Ivor."

But then you said: "I should never say the name Ivor to anyone."

(A moment between them. He's horrified.)

Oh my god is his name really Ivor?!

HELEN. Look, it just...came out.

JORIS. Helen, you can't say their actual names!!

You can't *know* their actual names!

How do you know his actual name?!

*(**HELEN** opens her mouth.)*

– Don't answer that. Actually don't answer that.

HELEN. I just –

JORIS. Oooh just don't for a second don't say anything.

This is bad, this is really bad.

(A beat.)

(This is not the case, but **HELEN** *tries it as a suggestion:)*

HELEN. You're overreacting?

JORIS. *(Comforting himself.)* He couldn't have told you his name. They never do that.

I've known Karl for five years and I know he's never once told me a real thing about himself.

HELEN. I knew Ivor back in Moscow. When I was studying abroad.

Before he started working for the whole...

Before *I* got really pulled into the whole...

JORIS. Oh god.

HELEN. And then *he* pulled *me* in, actually.

JORIS. He...?

HELEN. We had dated.

JORIS. Oh God.

HELEN. For two years and we were gonna get married –

JORIS. Oh GOD.

HELEN. – this was when I was still making my own movies.

And then he dumped me and then he joined the Bureau of Propaganda and then he called me in and I thought I was gonna be arrested because I was making some pretty weird shit back then at the time, like some really intense shit – but deeply cinematic –

(but also our break-up had been rocky, frankly)

but instead he was like: How Would You Like To Work For The Party.

And then he said Everyone Calls Me Gregor Now.

But obviously I knew his name was Ivor.

*(**JORIS** has been staring at her, open-mouthed.)*

What?

JORIS. *(Dazed.)* I have spent so long trying not to know anything I shouldn't.

*(This is the wrong answer. It is much less brave than **HELEN** would have hoped.)*

HELEN. Kidding.

JORIS. ...What?

HELEN. *(Flat.)* I was kidding.

JORIS. ...No you weren't.

Were you?

You weren't.

Were you?

HELEN. Made it all up. I'm still good for a cover story on the spur of the moment.

JORIS. Wait so

wait so

HELEN. Gotta keep you on your toes.

JORIS. *Is* there an Ivor?

(Straight to his face, but she's lying, isn't she? Is she?)

HELEN. There's no Ivor.

(A beat between them.)

(They study each other.)

(They have been together for some time and every once in a while they remember that they are complete strangers to each other in certain ways.)

JORIS. If you weren't kidding –

HELEN. I was.

JORIS. *(Spiraling a bit.)* Okay but if you weren't… I would want you to – to tell me

if there was something that involved me somehow –

if I was being handled by more than one handler, for example –

or if there were doubts, doubts in Moscow about me –

HELEN. Hey. Hey. Joris.

(He looks at her.)

You're OK. Everything is OK.

JORIS. We need to be able to trust each other. Don't we?

HELEN. Let's talk about Spain.

Three

(Time shifts.)

(Another night.)

*(**HELEN** and **JORIS** are having a nightcap/ brainstorming session. A big piece of butcher paper is stretched across the big wall.)*

JORIS. Sangria!

HELEN. Yes!

Bulls?

JORIS. That's on the list.

(He goes to the wall and underlines BULLS.)

HELEN. Paella!

JORIS. On the list.

(He underlines PAELLA.)

HELEN. *Don Quixote.*

JORIS. *(He's never read it.)* Right...

HELEN. As metaphor?

JORIS. "The insanity of the aristocracy."

HELEN. I think it's about chasing your dreams?

Dreams of working class liberation?

JORIS. I've never read *Don Quixote.*

HELEN. Ugh, me neither, it seemed boring.

Do we have time to read it?

JORIS. My Dinner Companion said we should be ready to make the movie fast.

HELEN. We should get someone who's read it to tell us about it.

JORIS. Flutes.

HELEN. Flutes?

JORIS. *(Suddenly uncertain.)* Flute music?

HELEN. ...Are flutes Spanish?

JORIS. Maybe not.

HELEN. Tambourines?

JORIS. Are tambourines Spanish?

HELEN. Guitars! *La guitarra!*

JORIS. *(Pensively.)* Guitars...

(They think but nobody writes anything.)

HELEN. Fiestas.

JORIS. *(An epiphany.)* SI-estas!!

HELEN. The naps?

JORIS. Afternoon naps. For everybody! Not just babies!

Super Spanish.

HELEN. *(Pitching the scene.)* "A late hot afternoon. Flies buzz. Bulls whip their...tails. And toss their horns. A farm. The working-class Spanish peasants are asleep, having their...

HELEN & JORIS. *(Together.) Siestas!"*

HELEN. "On the splintery wooden table in their homely kitchen: olives! Olive oil! An earthen jug of...*vino!"*

JORIS. *(How did I not think of that.)* "Vino"!

HELEN. "While the peasants sleep...the crushing machine of war rolls closer."

JORIS. *(Searching to replace "war.")* "The crushing machine of – of –"

HELEN. War.

JORIS. No, war is the good thing.

(Writes EL WAR. As he writes:)

War is the thing that will save the working people. War is the thing that we need the Americans to throw money at, in order to uphold values of – of humanism.

HELEN. No no

war and revolution are two different things.

It goes like: "War is terrible, war is coming, war is the Fascist boot crushing the noble poor, the noble poor must RISE UP! Rise up and stage a revolution!"

You see?

(A moment between them.)

*(**HELEN** is good at this. **JORIS** is a little unsettled.)*

(She writes: LA REVOLUCIÓN.)

JORIS. I… Yes, of course… When you put it like that, I can…

(A beat. He clears his throat. Onward!)

My Dinner Companion said that we should target Ernest.

HELEN. *(She doesn't like him.)* …Hemingway?

JORIS. He's very famous, obviously.

HELEN. Right…

JORIS. Mass commercial appeal. Ticket sales through the roof.

HELEN. Hmm.

JORIS. Girlfriend has ties to Roosevelt. Which is *huge.*

HELEN. His wife?

JORIS. No, the girlfriend, the new girlfriend, she's very close to Eleanor.

But most importantly you've got the whole – you know, the Voice Of America thing.

HELEN. Right...

*(**JORIS** can tell she is not saying that she hates him. But it's palpable.)*

JORIS. You don't like him.

*(**HELEN** shrugs.)*

My Dinner Companion said Moscow is *very* invested in Ernest.

HELEN. Great! Ernest. Love him.

Are we turning him?

JORIS. No no. He can't be seen as a Member.

He needs to stay – you know, *all-American.*

HELEN. Uh huh.

You know he can be...tricky.

JORIS. Tricky?

HELEN. Ornery.

Whatever you want him to do, he wants to do the opposite.

JORIS. I was thinking we could just...invite him over? To talk about...

HELEN. Spain?

JORIS. He likes Spain. A lot.

(Beat – he can tell **HELEN** *isn't buying this.)*

We shouldn't invite him over?

HELEN. Not at first.

If we want Ernest, we should invite John Dos Passos first.

JORIS. Dos? Isn't he a little bit...?

HELEN. What?

JORIS. I don't know...

Like. He thinks too much? And those stupid *glasses*?

HELEN. He's very In right now.

JORIS. If we want Ernest, we should call Ernest. What's Dos have to do with this?

HELEN. Friends with Ernest, twenty years,

this weird competitive friendship, haven't you seen them at parties?

Dos starts talking and Ernest has to interrupt.

Ernest starts talking, and Dos goes for a smoke.

JORIS. He does??

HELEN. Joris, you need to watch people more carefully.

JORIS. I watch people! I watch the people I'm targeting.

HELEN. Right, that's fifty percent of the people you should be watching.

You need to observe *everybody* at *every* second.

JORIS. I still don't see why we're talking about Dos.

HELEN. Dos has that whole Spain connection, backpacking as a youth,

fell in love with the red Spanish soil, the bright Spanish sun, etc, best and oldest friend is that intellectual aristocrat José Robles

so then Dos gets to be like: *My Spanish brother!* –

and the whole thing makes Ernest furious.

He's like, you were *backpacking* with a *pansy* while I was *slaughtering bulls.*

So if we approach Dos, and we ask him to write a screenplay for a big splashy film

about Spain

how do you imagine Ernest is gonna react?

JORIS. ...Jealous?

HELEN. Furious!

He's gonna be like: *Why didn't they ask me!*

He's gonna be like: *That should've been me!*

He's gonna be like: *Nobody is touching this goddamn movie except me!*

And there you go. Hooked.

(A beat.)

JORIS. ...You're good at this.

HELEN. I know.

JORIS. *(Insecure.)* Am I less good at this?

HELEN. You're a filmmaker. I'm a strategist.

JORIS. You're also a filmmaker.

HELEN. ...I was.

JORIS. You still are.

(He was trying to give her a gift with that one, and she feels it.)

HELEN. *(Moved.)* Thank you.

(Beat.)

JORIS. So – Dos first.

HELEN. Dos first.

(A moment. She has always liked Dos, in a genuine way. Maybe a tiny bit of a crush. And she can't help saying.)

And he's a nice guy.

*(**JORIS** looks at her, a little alarmed.)*

JORIS. A nice guy...?

HELEN. Of all of them, he's just like. A real person. You know?

He says what he means. He's just an absolutely decent human being in that whole circle of... well. People like us.

JORIS. *(Increasingly alarmed.)* Uh... Helen.

HELEN. We can *acknowledge* that he's *nice*, Joris, it's OK, we don't have to sacrifice the mission by acknowledging that he's nice. Sometimes you can just appreciate that people are exactly who they say they are, without you actually being who you say *you* are.

JORIS. *(Lying a bit; this got personal.)* Moscow is cautious about Dos.

(A beat.)

HELEN. Cautious?

JORIS. A little bit. I think.

HELEN. Cautious in what way cautious?

JORIS. It was sort of just a...vibe. I don't know.

HELEN. When has Dos ever come up?

JORIS. *(Lying.)* Recently. Recently.

HELEN. Did this come from Karl?

JORIS. I shouldn't have –

HELEN. What were his *exact* words.

JORIS. He didn't really –

words weren't really –

more like a…flicker of…

something in the mouth and the eyes…

*(**JORIS** overacts: glancing around, nervous.)*

I feel like we shouldn't…?

HELEN. Oh for God's sake, we're not *bugged.*

JORIS. *(Mouthing.)* (How Do You Know?)

*(Fine, let's get real. A little bit of a "fuck you" when **HELEN** says:)*

HELEN. Ivor told me.

OK?

No bugs in here.

We meet in here.

Sometimes. When you're out.

(A beat between them.)

(There's so much that could be said.)

(Like: what the fuck, Helen!)

(And: you meet him here?)

(And: so he's real??)

(What he can't stop himself from asking is:)

JORIS. Have you *slept* with him in here?

HELEN. Whoa. Joris.

JORIS. Have you fucked him in our *bed*?

HELEN. Joris, I want to caution you to take a deep breath and think very carefully before you keep talking.

JORIS. Because we *are* being bugged.

HELEN. No, because I will only put up with so much bullshit from a colleague before I walk out that door.

(A beat.)

JORIS. *(Small and miserable, but this question is so so honest.)* A colleague or a boyfriend?

HELEN. Both.

JORIS. But if you had to pick one?

HELEN. Both.

(Beat.)

JORIS. Do you still love him?

HELEN. What do you mean *still*?

JORIS. You were *together* for two years! You were going to get married! You joined the Party for love of him!

HELEN. Oh! No.

No no

I never joined the Party just like *you* never joined the Party

because I don't give a fuck about politics, as you well know,

I just work for them –

with them

for them –

because it became crystal clear that nobody was gonna let me make movies for a living so I needed a job

and honestly, infiltrating artistic circles and pitching the KGB slate is not a hard job

so this all just kind of came together and made a lot of sense as my next best step.

(A beat.)

JORIS. So you don't love him.

You do love him?

You did love him but you don't anymore?

You did and you still do but you love me more?

HELEN. *(So gently but so firmly: this conversation is finished.)* Let's start with Dos.

Four

(The wall opens or shifts to reveal: **JOHN DOS PASSOS.***)*

(Easygoing, decent, friendly, a little dorky. Maybe he's drinking a cold beer.)

DOS. Oh man okay well

Spain

what can I say.

It's great!

I've always liked Spain!

As a kid, a young man, my first solo trip led me to Spain:

Backpacking!

Art!

A night train!

I met my best friend on that night train

José Robles

It was 1916

we were both twenty-one

he comes from this big influential Spanish family but

he actually moved to Maryland and

now he teaches history at Johns Hopkins

which is hilarious to me, I'm like:

Pepe, you own fifty million acres and like a

hacienda, basically

or your family does, whatever,

what are you doing scrounging for tenure at Johns Hopkins??

But he's this total idealist

he's like: My Family Is Conservative, I'll Never Accept Their Blood Money

and I'm like:

(Genuinely impressed.)

"Okay, Pepe!"

(Anyway.)

How did I get to...

Oh! Spain! Yeah!

God it's such a great country. Everybody should go.

My first night in Madrid, back in our youth,

Pepe and I saw this flamenco dancer

I'll never forget it –

(Back in the moment –)

She was the greatest dancer in the world, this woman,

a Gypsy named Pastora Imperio

her dazzling footwork, her snapping fingers

the maroon flower at her breast,

she stares into my soul

she sees the roadmap of all that has led me here

and all that will lead me here again –

(Anyway.)

So yeah, Spain is great! I think it has a lot to teach us, honestly, as a nation.

Ernest likes to go on this whole *thing* about the bulls

– and sure, the bulls, okay! –

but the truth is, Spain is possessed of much subtler metaphors.

(He's serious now.)

Everybody can *see* bull-fighting, it's obvious.

What I'm trying to say is

the quieter stuff is also Spain.

The stuff you don't see right away.

The stuff you just feel, this vibration under the skin,

like the whole country is an engine and it's taking you somewhere.

(A little embarrassed.)

I don't know. What do I know.

(Shift.)

I was talking to Pepe a few weeks ago, before he left,

and he was like: Everybody's talking about this big Civil War

that seems to be happening

and I think I should go back to Spain.

And I was like: Pepe, I mean, I hear you, but also

you have tenure?

And he was like: Yeah but

everybody thinks things could finally change.

The conversations are finally different, even inside my own family.

If you're resisting Franco's army and tearing down a collaborating government and rebuilding your entire country,

well then,

why not rebuild in a totally new way?

They collectivized factories in Catalonia!

They turned the Ritz into a worker canteen in Barcelona!

Pepe was like: what if this is the Great Revolution I've always been waiting for

and now it's here

and I'm in Maryland grading papers?

Which made *me* think.

Honestly

What am *I* doing?

But *then* I thought:

whenever people start to get all excited about one kind of war vs another kind of war

you just have to sort of

stop for a second

and ask yourself

what are we doing, exactly?

Like, which kind of war doesn't leave hundreds of thousands of bodies in its wake?

I mean whatever you're saying the war is *for*...

it's still...a war. You know?

So –

but –

that's not a thing that people like hearing.
Especially when they already got themselves excited.
Especially when they're already writing novels
and poems and songs and essays
and making movies
about this particular War.
Which I guess –
if I've answered all your questions,
that leads me to *my* question
which is:
why are *you*
making a movie
about *Spain*?

Five

*(**DOS** remains where he is, as lights snap up on **HELEN**, in the living room.)*

*(She and **DOS** are in the middle of a casual and slightly flirtatious nightcap.)*

(There is a real chemistry between them.)

HELEN. I've always liked you.

DOS. Well, thanks.

HELEN. Always thought you were smart. Smarter than the rest of your friends, honestly.

DOS. *(But it's a joke.)* I've always thought that as well.

HELEN. See? Like that! Just now –

you were making fun of *yourself* when you said that

instead of making fun of *them.*

Whereas if Ernest had said that exact same sentence

he would have meant it.

DOS. Well, Ernest has always had a deep belief in his own abilities.

HELEN. And you?

DOS. I try to have deep convictions instead of deep beliefs.

HELEN. The difference being –?

DOS. You have to keep testing your convictions.

HELEN. See?

I like you.

(Is she flirting? He isn't sure. He's attracted to her, and also trying to not get himself in trouble.)

DOS. Well, I appreciate that, Helen.

(A beat.)

Where's your man Joris?

HELEN. Oh, he's out at the moment. Somebody's gallery opening, I forget who.

DOS. You didn't want to go?

HELEN. What do I know about art?

DOS. Nobody knows anything about art, but it's a great excuse to dress up and drink.

Both of which you're quite good at.

HELEN. Oh have you noticed?

(A slightly charged beat. That got flirty.)

DOS. So the movie...

HELEN. Yes, the movie.

DOS. Has Joris been to Spain?

HELEN. We both feel very connected to Spain.

*(**DOS** isn't sure what to make of this answer.)*

DOS. But you...? [know Spain well?]

Have you...? [been to Spain?]

HELEN. What even *is* Spain?

(A beat.)

We'd like you to write the screenplay.

DOS. Me!

HELEN. Your name came up. We were both quite excited by you.

DOS. That's a first.

HELEN. No false modesty please, you were all over the magazine covers –

DOS. A few months ago. It came and went fairly quickly. My new book came out and suddenly I was a face you could put on a cover. But I don't think anybody actually *read* the book – everybody thinks I'm weird and boring – but it was a book that was great to mention *as if* you'd read it.

HELEN. I don't think you're boring.

DOS. Have you read my books?

HELEN. ...No.

DOS. See?

HELEN. They're long.

DOS. Well, fair.

HELEN. And you don't do plot, you do like – linguistic experiments.

DOS. *(Pleased.)* That's exactly right! That's what I would've said myself.

...But you don't like linguistic experiments?

HELEN. I'm more interested in visual experiments.

Language is just a vehicle for deceit.

DOS. You can lie with an image much faster and more cleanly than you lie with a sentence.

HELEN. Writers love to make this argument.

DOS. *(Laughing.)* But it's true!

Those photos of Ernest in the bull ring, sleeves rolled up?

He jumped down into the dust, got his picture taken, and jumped back up into the stands.

But you see those pictures and you think – *What a man!*

You know? *What a goddamn man.*

Because when you see a picture, you think you were *there*. But I was *actually* there, that particular afternoon. The truth and the picture are very different.

HELEN. You don't like him that much, do you.

DOS. *(Dryly.)* We're old friends.

(Beat.)

My point! Is not about Ernest. My point is...

I forget my point.

(Flirting, just a little.)

Maybe that you should read my books.

HELEN. Maybe you should write my movie. Since you understand so much about lying with an image.

DOS. I'm hoping that nothing in your movie would require lying.

HELEN. I was joking.

(A beat. They study each other.)

(Something in **HELEN** *longs to reveal itself to him.)*

You know, I was a filmmaker. Back in the day.

DOS. Aren't you still?

HELEN. Please. You know *Joris* is the filmmaker, and I'm his girlfriend, and everybody pretends to believe us when we say that we collaborate. But what they think it really means is that Joris makes movies and I show up to parties on his arm.

*(**DOS** is quiet, embarrassed, because yeah that is what everybody thinks, and honestly that's what he thought too. **HELEN** sees this.)*

HELEN. Right.

Thank you for not protesting. I appreciate the honesty.

DOS. Look, I just – I mean I don't know a lot about film, so –

HELEN. No, it's fine, it's quite all right.

I *don't* make movies anymore, that's the truth.

I do all the things one does in order to make movies – I organize things, I talk to people, I bring money and artists into the same room – but then in the end, I don't make the movies.

DOS. Why don't you?

HELEN. Come on.

DOS. No really.

HELEN. Don't you just assume it's because I don't have anything to say?

DOS. ...No, I don't assume that.

HELEN. Why not?

DOS. Because I can see how much you miss it.

(A beat between them. Electricity.)

*(When **HELEN** answers, it is with a growing intensity and vulnerability – she is, in her own way, laying herself bare.)*

HELEN. What if I told you I was performing a service that was greater than art.

DOS. I would ask what that was.

HELEN. People think they have their own ideas

or that ideas just...appear in the world around them organically.

But what if I said, the thoughts you have are being formed, shaped, designed to meet a set of specifications, and then *served* to you.

You aren't *having* a thought, you're *receiving* the thought that someone else crafted for you.

DOS. ...Are you still talking about art?

HELEN. Let's say I'm talking about...producing.

DOS. That you're Joris's producer, you mean?

HELEN. Yes but no. Not quite, but yes.

*(**DOS** can sense that **HELEN** has become agitated, although he doesn't know why.)*

DOS. Are you –?

HELEN. I'm just a piece of a machine. A cog in the works.

I'm a tiny little spoon that carries a ball bearing three inches to the left then drops it.

You know? Nobody would say "that tiny little spoon is doing such a great job."

But if the ball bearing reaches the place it's supposed to go, that's because of the tiny spoon.

In part. In part.

DOS. I don't think I'm following you...

HELEN. I'm mixing metaphors.

DOS. Are you OK?

HELEN. Of course.

*(**DOS** studies her, troubled, but not sure why.)*

DOS. OK… Are you sure?

HELEN. Why wouldn't I be OK?

DOS. I don't know.

I guess…

I guess probably you're OK.

(He continues to study her.)

HELEN. You should probably head out, let me get some sleep.

DOS. Did I –?

Did I say something wrong just now?

HELEN. Of course not. I just got quite tired.

Can we count on you for the screenplay, darling?

DOS. You can count on me.

HELEN. We'll have you and Ernest over for lunch.

DOS. …Ernest?

HELEN. Just a lovely lunch, where we all talk about Spain.

Six

(The wall reveals: **KARL.***)*

(We can't yet see his features clearly. He might be largely in shadow, though his mouth is prominent and clearly lit.)

(There is something bleak and claustrophobic and sad about the moment we catch him in. He is stealing a moment away from the crushing bureaucratic machine of his day-job...for the Bureau of Propaganda.)

(A breath.)

(He hums.)

(He sings an operatic phrase.)

(This is a man who loves opera.)

(In his youth, he dreamed of being an opera singer. He has given up on that dream, but these are still the fantasies that sustain him now.)

(And he has an incredible voice.)

(A red phone rings.)

(Now is no longer the time for opera.)

(He is summoned, away from his escape, back to the machine inside which he functions.)

Seven

(Gathered together in the living room: **ERNEST, DOS, HELEN, JORIS.***)*

*(***ERNEST** *has a keen awareness under his bombast. He isn't as tipsy as he seems nor as oblivious. He enjoys performing his persona, but that doesn't mean he can't see you sharply from beneath it. He is someone who hates himself almost as much as he wants your love, and it makes him unpredictable.)*

(Everybody has already been here for a long time, as **JORIS** *and* **HELEN** *work to wrangle* **ERNEST.***)*

(Multiple bottles are open.)

JORIS. The thing about our little movie, honestly –

ERNEST. *(Sonorous and with intention.)* War.

(Nobody knows what to say. He does it again.)

War.

Is the only thing worth making work about

for a man.

JORIS. Yes, and –

ERNEST. And Joris...is a Man!

And a movie about War. Is a movie about Men.

DOS. Well, the way I see it –

ERNEST. Joris is the real deal. Man can drink all night.

JORIS. Well, that's very –

ERNEST. Reminds me of Spain, honestly. They can drink!

JORIS. Yes! Spain! You know, the thing about the Spanish farmers –

ERNEST. And their *joie de vivre*! Which is French, but you know what I mean.

HELEN. It's hard to have joie de vivre when you're crushed beneath the boot of Fascism these days. Which is what our movie's about.

DOS. As the writer, I'm approaching this as sort of a –

ERNEST. *(Not listening.)* Joy that's aligned with a proximity to death.

Which brings us back to War.

A Man At War experiences Eros in a whole new way.

HELEN. *(To* **JORIS.***)* I need a drink, darling. Or several.

(To **DOS.***)* Do you need a drink?

*(**JORIS** refills **HELEN**'s glass while she refills **DOS**'s.)*

JORIS. *(To* **ERNEST.***)* The thing is, Ernest, the movie needs those of us who just – understand Spain so well and so clearly.

*(Remembers **DOS** exists.)*

All of us, I mean, present company!

(Back to **ERNEST.***)*

Someone who has *been* to Spain, who has felt the red Spanish soil under his fingernails, who has broken bread at the tables of the laughing, dying farmers, men whose connections to the land itself –

ERNEST. And the women!

HELEN. Yes do tell us about the women, Ernest.

Do they have dazzling footwork and snapping fingers?

*(**DOS** shoots a glance at her, she smirks but keeps going without looking at him:)*

Do they stare into your soul?

ERNEST. Yes, by God yes. I feel like I'm there right now!

HELEN. Ooh, me too.

JORIS. *(It's like herding cats.)* – So in thinking about a man who can speak for the people

a man who is a man among men

a man *of* the men

(What is he even saying?)

a man whose hu-*man*-ity is, uh,

really we just began to think of you, Ernest.

DOS. Who?

HELEN. And Dos.

JORIS. Yes of course and Dos.

*(**DOS** realizes now exactly how he's being used.)*

DOS. *(Dry as a bone.)* Yes of course.

*(**ERNEST** turns to **DOS**. There's old competition here.)*

ERNEST. We go way back, Dos and me.

DOS. Way back.

ERNEST. All the way. Young men together. He's known several of my wives. Not Biblically.

DOS. No, not Biblically.

ERNEST. He likes my current wife the best, isn't that right Dos?

DOS. You know I do.

ERNEST. Likes my girlfriend a little bit less. The current one.

DOS. Ernest...

ERNEST. Called her a "blonde floozy," I think.

DOS. I don't recall saying that.

ERNEST. Maybe you just thought it. Maybe I just looked at your face and saw you think it.

(Back to **JORIS** *and* **HELEN**, *performing.)*

You know, the Spanish – speaking of the Spanish – the Spanish understand that a man can't fall in love only once. A man falls in love – and then he falls in love again! A man is capable of many loves. That doesn't render his marriage any *less*.

DOS. I beg to differ, Ernest, the Spanish *pioneered* the concept of fiercely loyal –

ERNEST. *(Cutting through him, to* **HELEN.***)* If Joris loved another girl, would that mean he loved you less? No! It would mean he was an artist, a passionate artist –

JORIS. Okay, Ernest, let's –

(But **HELEN** *dives into the fray, with intensity. She is in her own way defending* **DOS** *– she feels bad for how they've used him.)*

HELEN. Fuck love.

ERNEST. *(Astonished.)* Fuck...love?

HELEN. Fuck it. Who cares?

ERNEST. Who cares...about *love*?

HELEN. Nothing is ever about love, Ernest, it's about power.

If Joris fucked another girl, what he would be communicating to me is that he believes that he has the power to dictate the terms of our relationship. When a man has a wife and a girlfriend, what he's communicating is that he has the *power* to rewrite social mores. And, by refusing to listen to a goddamn thing Joris has been saying for the last two hours, what *you're* demonstrating is that you have the power to dismiss us to our faces, and we'll still keep trying to seduce you.

Or did you think it was because we loved you?

(A shocked beat. And then **ERNEST** *reacts, completely delighted.)*

ERNEST. God, she's like a bracing wind, isn't she.

She's like the sharp end of a knife.

JORIS. Ummm...

ERNEST. *(Genuine.)* A woman like a blast of shrapnel. Nothing beats a woman like that.

HELEN. *(Genuine.)* Thank you.

ERNEST. You are *very* welcome. What's this fucking movie you're so excited about?

JORIS & HELEN. Spain!

DOS. ...Spain.

ERNEST. Spain! Great. I'm in.

Eight

(The wall opens or shifts to reveal: **IVOR**. *In the shadows. As with the first time we saw him, he is less visually accessible even than* **KARL** *– more hidden and atmospheric.)*

(Perhaps a hat covers most of his face.)

(Perhaps he might be smoking; smoke rising and curling around his face.)

(Either way, the atmosphere **IVOR** *lives in is: dangerous spy thriller, understated, not cheesy.)*

(He passes past **HELEN***'s world and vanishes as we see:)*

*(***HELEN** *in the living room, staring at the butcher paper. Words about Spain have been replaced with index cards, notes, images – preparation for a film taking shape.)*

*(***JORIS** *bursts in, thrilled and full of energy.)*

JORIS. Hello hello!

HELEN. How was it?

JORIS. Moscow is *very* pleased about Ernest.

HELEN. Oh good.

JORIS. I was getting ready to tell Our Dinner Companion about Ernest, but before I could even say anything, he said:

(With significance.)

Good Job.

HELEN. Oh wow.

JORIS. And get this: our Dinner Companion mentioned Ernest to *his* Dinner Companion –

HELEN. Already?

JORIS. Already! And *his* Dinner Companion said:

(Even more significant.)

Good Job.

And then Karl said we can make it two hours long.

HELEN. ...You're kidding.

JORIS. One hundred and twenty minutes. If we want.

HELEN. That's...expensive.

JORIS. Karl said: don't worry about it.

HELEN. You just called him Karl. Twice.

*(**JORIS** realizes that maybe his excitement made him over-bold.)*

JORIS. And then Our Dinner Companion lit my cigar –

HELEN. He lit your cigar?

JORIS. – and he said: *Think about the next one, Joris.*

HELEN. The next one...

JORIS. *(Obviously.)* The next movie.

HELEN. ...After this.

JORIS. That's what "next" means. He said: *Think about Italy.*

HELEN. What about Italy?!

JORIS. Just to think about it.

If we keep going the way we're going, you could call this a two-picture deal.

Maybe more! Maybe more.

We're in the big leagues now!

(This information lands on **HELEN**. *Briefly, behind her eyes, she watches the years roll out ahead of her. Movie after movie. Inside this machine.)*

HELEN. Ernest hasn't written anything yet.

JORIS. I'm sure he's been writing a *little.*

HELEN. Ernest hasn't been writing a little because he's been drinking a lot.

JORIS. Maybe he's just not ready to share. I was making a shot-list and I was thinking – POV: ant. You know? I'm an ant in the dirt, the rich noble dirt.

HELEN. Hmm...

JORIS. Or maybe: POV Raindrop. Right? I fall on the face of a weary soldier.

HELEN. What did Karl think?

JORIS. We didn't get into details but...he didn't seem particularly excited by Dos.

Maybe we should detach him.

HELEN. What? No!

JORIS. We don't need him anymore. You said use him to get Ernest, and we got Ernest.

HELEN. We need Dos.

JORIS. Dos isn't additive. Come on, you might dislike Ernest, but he's our ticket.

HELEN. I don't dislike him.

JORIS. No?

HELEN. It's not about *him.* It's just – men like that...who get *handed* things...

Some of us work so hard and we never get handed those things.

JORIS. *(A little defensive.)* I've worked for everything I have.

HELEN. I wasn't –

JORIS. I'm not saying certain things aren't easier for me, as a man, but I've worked –

HELEN. I wasn't saying *You.*

Joris, I don't mean you, I don't want *your* career.

JORIS. *(Hurt.)* ...Oh.

HELEN. ...That came out wrong.

JORIS. What's so wrong with my career?

HELEN. No, nothing, I just –

JORIS. I'm making a living –

HELEN. *(Can't help herself.)* You're making propaganda.

JORIS. So are you!!

HELEN. I know! I know that!! Did I say I wanted *my* career?!

(A fragile silence. **JORIS** *is deeply hurt.)*

JORIS. Helen...

HELEN. I'm tired.

JORIS. It doesn't have to be hard. We don't have to overthink this.

HELEN. I'm just tired.

JORIS. Do you want me to go back to making five minute movies?

HELEN. I'm not saying –

JORIS. We did everything you said and it worked! Why aren't you happy?

(A beat. As honest as she's ever gotten:)

HELEN. We never talk about this anymore, Joris, because mostly we just talk about the details – but when Karl introduced us...you had so many things you wanted to make. And not all of them involved Russian talking points. You know?

(...And now it's getting a little dangerous.)

JORIS. *(A warning.)* Helen... If anyone heard you...

HELEN. Are you going to turn me in?

JORIS. No! Of course not, no.

(A beat.)

How can you even ask me that!

HELEN. If Karl asked you...

If he ever asked you if you've heard me say anything...

JORIS. I wouldn't turn you in!

HELEN. So you'd lie to him? You'd lie to his face?

JORIS. *(Thrown.)* I... I mean...

HELEN. You know what happens if you lie to them.

JORIS. I wouldn't lie to him, but...

HELEN. So you'd tell him the truth.

JORIS. No! No. I would try not to say anything.

HELEN. You'd try not to say anything.

*(**JORIS** can feel that he's failing her.)*

JORIS. I would try not to say anything that was a lie and I would try not to say anything that was true.

HELEN. But where does that leave you?

(A silence. **JORIS** *is stumped. He has no idea.)*

(A real question, and a dangerous one:)

JORIS. What are you really asking me?

HELEN. Are you sure this is worth it?

Nine

*(***JORIS***,* **HELEN** *and* **ERNEST** *sit around the apartment. It has been turned into a writers' room – think whiteboard, etc. Mid-conversation.* **ERNEST** *drinks throughout.)*

ERNEST. Nobody cares about ants.

JORIS. My point is –

ERNEST. This is a movie about *men.*

JORIS. Yes but –

ERNEST. Sweating, dying men.

*(***JORIS** *opens his mouth to argue but* **HELEN** *steps in, brokering –)*

HELEN. I think Joris is just saying there's an incredible opportunity here –

ERNEST. We want to be so close to a man that his sweat is our sweat.

JORIS. *(Hopefully.)* You know, I had this image the other day where – okay, we're a raindrop –

ERNEST. Raindrops and ants??

(He takes a huge gulp, with gusto.)

HELEN. Did you happen to bring any pages with you?

ERNEST. Pages?

HELEN. Of the screenplay.

ERNEST. Pages...

HELEN. Of the first half of the screenplay that you thought you might have last Monday.

ERNEST. Screenplay pages...

(He drinks.)

(They wait.)

(He gets up and walks over to the bar cart to refill his drink.)

HELEN. Are there no pages?

JORIS. *(Sotto.)* Helen...

ERNEST. I have pages.

(With a wicked smile, he taps his forehead.)

In here.

HELEN. Okay, well, we do need them in a format we can read. And show.

ERNEST. Show?

HELEN. Our...financier wants to see something.

ERNEST. What does money know of art?

(He tosses back his drink, but this phrase sort of charms him, and he plays with it:)

Hmm

What does...*money*...know of WAR?

What does...*power*...know of...*money*?

Hm no

What do *soldiers* know of *love*?

(He looks at them: Aha!)

*(**HELEN** shakes her head. **ERNEST** shrugs.)*

What do soldiers know of...irrigation?

JORIS. ...Irrigation?

(Really seeing it – with a kind of awe and beauty:)

ERNEST. Water is life.

War is death.

We start in the scorched Spanish fields.

We need water!

But our farmers must become soldiers. Death will flow through these fields like the rain.

HELEN. *(Slowly.)* Not bad.

*(**ERNEST** pretends to ignore her, but this compliment is actually fuel to him.)*

ERNEST. I've got it all up here.

– What money?

JORIS. Sorry?

ERNEST. You said financier so...who's the money?

*(**JORIS** and **HELEN** flicker a glance to each other.)*

HELEN. *(With a laugh.)* I'm terrible with names, darling.

*(They wait nervously as **ERNEST** tops up his drink –)*

ERNEST. Money...

What does...*money*...know of PLEASURE?

And the answer of course: is quite a lot.

(He laughs and drinks.)

*(**JORIS** opens his mouth, **HELEN** gestures to him not to speak, and **DOS** walks in...with a bouquet of bodega flowers.)*

HELEN. Dos!

JORIS. Dos!

ERNEST. Oh... Dos.

DOS. ...I thought we were starting in half an hour.

ERNEST. Nice flowers.

DOS. I thought I was early.

HELEN. *(With an easy laugh.)* Oh, we all just got here.

DOS. Well...

This is for you.

(He gives **HELEN** *the flowers.)*

*(***JORIS** *can't help being irritated, and* **ERNEST** *clocks this, and the two men share a sort of weirdly brotherly eyeroll about* **DOS** *as –)*

HELEN. Oh that's so lovely! You shouldn't have!

DOS. I just saw them on the way here and I thought of you.

JORIS. Well thank you very much, Dos.

HELEN. I'll just get a vase. Oh and let me take your coat.

(She does, and heads off.)

JORIS. Make yourself at home.

DOS. I must've gotten the time wrong.

JORIS. No no

you're right on time.

*(***ERNEST** *has poured two drinks –)*

ERNEST. Drink, old boy?

DOS. I'm all right.

ERNEST. Okay.

(– And he takes both back to his seat.)

JORIS. OK! Let's get started!

ERNEST. Where were we?

*(**HELEN** returns with a vase, into which she fits the flowers –)*

HELEN. Oh we were just chatting about the start of the film –

DOS. Horses.

HELEN & JORIS. Horses?

DOS. I was thinking – a galloping herd of horses. Racing toward the camera.

HELEN. *(Entertaining it.)* Oh...

JORIS. *(Not entertaining it.)* Uh...

DOS. Sorry I didn't mean to interrupt, I just got excited.

HELEN. That could be...dynamic.

ERNEST. Eleanor mentioned she'd love to host a screening when we're ready.

DOS. Eleanor?

ERNEST. ...Roosevelt.

*(This is a masterful play and **DOS** knows it.)*

JORIS & HELEN. Ohh... / wow –

ERNEST. Dos, what were you saying about horses?

DOS. *(Rallies.)* I mean I had a few ideas.

I've been spending some time with Goya – just really taking in what he does with darkness and light – and human suffering –

JORIS. Sure, right...

ERNEST. Goya was deaf.

DOS. I'm sorry?

ERNEST. And blind.

DOS. ...Um. Okay –

ERNEST. *(Stirring his ice loudly with a little smirk.)* I know about Goya too.

HELEN. Would anybody like a drink?

ERNEST. *(With pleasure, taking his time.)* The thing about you, old boy...

DOS. What's the thing about me, Ernest?

ERNEST. You like to make things complicated. I like to keep them simple.

DOS. I prefer the word "nuanced."

ERNEST. Things are hard enough already!

DOS. The thing about *you*, old boy.

ERNEST. Ooh tell me.

JORIS. Gentlemen! Gentlemen...

DOS. You want people to feel like they don't need to be any smarter or better. You just want them to love you.

ERNEST. Maybe they're smart enough. There's a reason nobody wants to read your books.

JORIS. Why don't we start with the Spanish fields?

HELEN. Yes, the fields!

*(**DOS** is stymied and frustrated.)*

DOS. I think I just have a few questions.

I've been thinking about this and I'm not entirely sure I understand the brief.

Maybe this is too *complicated*, Ernest, but – What exactly are we saying about Spain?

(This is a dangerous question. And the wrong question.)

HELEN. Well, darling –

ERNEST. Spain is a battleground.

DOS. I mean politically – it's intricate. Isn't it?

JORIS. I wouldn't say / it's *intricate...*

DOS. My friend José Robles is in Madrid right now – I just got a letter from him – and he says he's surrounded by *Russians.*

ERNEST. Russians?

HELEN. Russians...?

JORIS. I'm sure that's not anything – [to worry about!]

DOS. In the Ministry of Foreign Affairs.

*(**JORIS** shoots **HELEN** a look –)*

HELEN. Oh that's fascinating.

DOS. José says he keeps running into them but none of the Spanish officials will exactly...you know, talk about it. Like kind of a secret, but if you know, you know. So it makes me ask: who's *actually* behind all this?

JORIS. I really don't think –

DOS. You know? Who's pulling the strings?

ERNEST. This is a movie called SPAIN. Not RUSSIA.

JORIS. *(Alarmed and steering them hastily back.)* You're right, Ernest! It's definitely about Spain!

ERNEST. Here's the thing.

Spain is a *metaphor*

because all places are metaphor

so the thing we should really be asking

is:

how

are *we*

Spain?

(He looks around them triumphantly.)

DOS. I'm sorry?

ERNEST. All of us.

DOS. *All* of us?

ERNEST. We are all Spain. *But how?*

And there's your movie.

(Inside the wall, a door that we have never before seen...creaks open. A shaft of light. It reveals a recording booth built into the wall.)

*(**ERNEST** is charmed and pleased. This is for him!)*

(He walks over...and steps inside.)

*(**JORIS** and **HELEN** are surprised by this:)*

JORIS. Oh!

HELEN. Oh what's that?

JORIS. Ernest?

(The door to the recording booth closes in his face.)

(The blinds open.)

DOS. Is that a recording booth?

JORIS. Well...

(The microphone appears: THUNK!)

*(**ERNEST** clicks the mic on, taps it firmly with his finger.)*

ERNEST. **Testing...testing...**

*(**DOS** is so upset about **ERNEST** that he gives up on caring about the sudden appearance of the recording booth.)*

DOS. *(Tightly to **JORIS**.)* Isn't this moving a little fast? What's he going to record?

JORIS. Ah – well – uh – truth be told –

DOS. We haven't written anything yet!

ERNEST. **Testing! Testing!**

(He blows into the mic and it makes a horrible windy crackle. Everyone covers their ears.)

DOS. And for that matter, I was under the impression that *I* was to write the screenplay!

JORIS. *(To **DOS**, flailing.)* Ah, yes, well

things are so

mutable!

Sometimes

DOS. You *asked* me –!

ERNEST. **Testingggggggggggg one two THREE!**

JORIS. It just sort of seems that

urgency is the uh

word du jour?

ERNEST. **check! check! check! soundCHECK!**

DOS. You said if Ernest had *ideas* –

but you expressly told *me* –

JORIS. you know

in future versions one could certainly –

ERNEST. **Annnnnd TESTING!**

(**ERNEST** *starts retrieving and stacking up bottles of alcohol in the window of the recording booth: whiskey, champagne, white wine, some French beer – he seems to be in possession of an endless supply of booze. He arranges the bottles around his work area.)*

HELEN. I mean you're *very* important to this project, Dos, obviously –

DOS. What is he gonna record?!

ERNEST. *(Into the mic, with feedback.)* – **Dos asked.**

(They look at him. He's unfazed.)

DOS. Excuse me...

ERNEST. – **Dos Passos said.**

DOS. ...Are you going to stay in there?

ERNEST. – **Dos Passos asked.**

DOS. Stop that.

ERNEST. – **Dos said.**

DOS. I'm not kidding!

ERNEST. **– Dos whined.**

DOS. I'm not whining!

ERNEST. **– Dos squealed.**

DOS. Oh my God. He's too much. He's always been too much.

This is what you get when you invite this man to do anything, you just get TOO MUCH all the time until it's over.

(A beat. They all wait for **ERNEST** *to narrate something. Instead, he's struck by what* **DOS** *said.)*

(He hears it. He takes it to heart. He clears his throat and leans into the mic.)

ERNEST. **Ernest can be too much.**

Ten

*(**ERNEST** is alone inside his recording booth. He is lit up. He speaks to us, through his mic. He might emerge from the recording booth as he speaks, but if so, he takes the mic with him.)*

(This should feel quiet and intimate and real, as opposed to his Narrator Voice.)

(He is cracked open. He is not performing.)

ERNEST. **He knows it about himself. He really can be.**

He isn't saying this as an excuse.

He is too much to himself as well.

One gets used to being a certain kind of a person.

To being *seen* as a certain kind of person.

Oh, let's call it a persona.

And then one starts to perform that persona all the time –

people get alarmed if they perceive you in some other state,

but then also eventually when you're with your wife –

and then eventually when you're alone.

And you start to feel a real fatigue, a complete exhaustion

with whatever this creature is that you're constantly performing

it just gets confusing and then you can't sleep

you have insomnia night after night

and you stop writing

and you stop reading

and you start to realize

what you're having

is what one might call a crisis of faith.

In the olden days, when there was a God,

you would have called it that.

(A beat. This is honest and raw. Unadorned.)

The craziest thing happened to me in Spain one summer.

And ever since I started working on this movie, I've been thinking about it.

I know you think I'm gonna talk about the bulls but

I'm not gonna talk about the bulls.

I met this woman,

a Spanish poet, in Pamplona for the feria –

and one night, very late at night, we were at the hotel bar and

she told me about a special kind of song, a very old and simple melody,

there are only a handful of people who still know it

and they all come from the same small ancient town

which is her hometown.

When you sing this song, you reach into somebody else's body.

What I mean is, the person who hears your song becomes...you, sort of.

For a time. You are inside them.

I said, That's ridiculous –

(but I was taking notes)

And she said, Do you want to try?

She said: There's no harm, is there?

And she was laughing, so I started laughing

(we were a bit drunk)

and I thought we were going to go to her room.

But instead, she just leaned across the bar between us, looking straight into my eyes and she started to hum.

Very low. She was humming so quietly and leaning so close, and even though the bar had been noisy, the background chaos began to drain away, and then –

I don't know how to say this –

I could *feel* her.

Like a tendril of something new

slipping inside me.

Like when you drink water that's so cold you feel it wending its way down your throat and into your stomach.

Like something that isn't you, but now it *is* you.

She was inside my face. She was looking out from my eyes.

She was looking at *herself* with *my* eyes!

And she looked different! Or – no, I mean

she looked at places I hadn't looked at –

her eyebrows and her chin and her forehead –

I'd looked at her lips and her eyes

(and the top of her tits)

(which you could sort of see through her shirt) –

I had constructed an image of lips and eyes and tit-tops but

she looked at her own earlobes, she looked at her own frown-lines

she looked down at her hands, on the bar

all of this with my eyes, using my eyes

and I was...her

and also myself, still

but also...her.

And then she looked at *me*.

Or – I looked at myself, with my eyes, which were *her* eyes

because she was using them, at that moment –

I looked at myself in the mirror hanging behind the bar

and I saw myself in a way that...

My face was pocked and pitted, hair in strange places,

jowly but also gaunt...

It was the face of a man who has turned himself into a *type* of man.

I looked at my face with our shared eyes and I saw things that

shook me, shook me to my core,

but also...

She thought I was beautiful, in certain ways – the lines of my jaw or

the look that I was wearing just then, startled and pained and a little scared –

I had never thought of myself as beautiful.

I have thought of myself in a lot of ways, as a lot of things

but that word has never once entered my head.

And then she stopped humming.

And she pulled out from behind my eyes

and it was just me again. Alone.

And she looked at me, she was laughing, she said: Did you feel anything?

But she knew that I did. She was there. She knew that I did.

A week passed. And I couldn't get what had happened out of my head.

I couldn't remember the melody, even though it had been so simple.

I looked for her in the bar, in the hotel, I asked friends about her

but I couldn't find her.

And then one day I ran into a friend of mine who knew her –

a dissipated British baron –

and I ended up telling him about that night with her

and the ancient song from her hometown

and how she'd climbed behind my eyes –

And my friend, he started laughing.

He said: Oh she tells that story to everyone.

He said: Her hometown? Is Madrid.

He said: You wanna know where that story came from?

We were all drinking late (he said) and telling ghost stories (he said)

and she came up with that one, and now she goes around and she just says it to every man she wants to fuck.

There's no song. There's no "*special ancient*" –

and I knew he was wrong.

I mean, he was *right*, factually he was right (it turns out)

but also he was wrong.

Because what happened that night? Inside me? was real.

I *saw* differently and so – for a brief interlude – I became different.

(Beat.)

It's like neuro-surgery. Isn't it? Art-making, story-telling.

You get inside somebody's brain and you rifle around and you change the connections,

you change the neural pathways, and then you change *them*.

And maybe? You save their life.

So this movie? That we're all doing?

It's the equivalent of radical brain surgery.

*(***ERNEST** *retreats back inside his sound booth.)*

Eleven

(Shift.)

*(**KARL** is revealed to us.)*

*(**KARL** is preparing to go to the opera. He puts on a tuxedo jacket and ties his tie.)*

*(**JORIS** makes his report. He's nervous but trying to act normal.)*

*(In the sound booth, **ERNEST** is at the typewriter working. Sometimes he lifts a page and reads to himself.)*

JORIS. – Really on track, I think you'll be quite pleased,

Ernest is writing and narrating,

Dos Passos is only, uh, consulting

I know I mentioned the Roosevelts

and

uh

we should be able to head to Spain next month.

*(**KARL** is frighteningly silent.)*

– or sooner! Even. Much sooner.

*(**KARL** says nothing. **JORIS** panics a little.)*

Uh, and we've been very careful to, you know, make sure that the focus stays simple

(just like you said)

like: you know –

ERNEST. *(Dramatic narration voice.)* **This Spanish earth is dry and hard.**

JORIS. Ernest had this whole idea where it's like: *we* language, *us* language,

like he'll talk as if he's a noble farmer, and he'll talk to the audience like *they're* noble farmers because "we" language is –

ERNEST. **sticky**

JORIS. it sticks to you, you know?

(Nothing from **KARL. JORIS** *is getting panicky.)*

Okay! What else! What else can I tell you.

We're thinking the movie begins with a choir singing

and then we follow some farmers into battle –

– And then we'll wrap it up with some kinda noble –

ERNEST. *(Narrating.)* **The young men who had never fought before...fight on.**

JORIS. – and there we are!

We'll have Moscow sign off on the draft, of course.

(Checks his watch.)

I know you're headed to the opera so I wouldn't want to delay you at all but...

Are there... Do you have any...questions?

(A beat.)

*(***KARL*** stands. The gesture should be shocking.)*

(He turns on **JORIS.***)*

(He might approach him – slowly, powerfully.)

(He speaks to **JORIS** *evenly and forcefully, in Russian.)*

(The only phrase we understand [unless we speak Russian] is the name Dos Passos, but it should be said in a tone that conveys a strong refusal.)

KARL. *(In Russian.)* DOS PASSOS is a problem.*

DOS PASSOS thinks too much

DOS PASSOS speaks Spanish

DOS PASSOS eats too many vegetables

DOS PASSOS drinks in moderate ways

and men who drink moderately can't be trusted – like DOS PASSOS!

Goodbye DOS PASSOS

Get rid of DOS PASSOS

No to DOS PASSOS!

(He exits.)

(A moment. **JORIS** *blinks, stunned.)*

*(***JORIS** *exits.)*

*(***HELEN** *enters.)*

(A new panel opens. This is **IVOR***.)*

(He stands, silhouetted against the light.)

(He turns his head. Looks at her. A summons.)

---

* For a Russian translation of this speech, see the Appendix at the back of this Acting Edition.

(Trepidatious, **HELEN** *straightens her clothing.)*

(She lifts her chin.)

(She marches toward the wall…and a door opens.)

(She steps into the wall, and is swallowed by it.)

(A beat.)

(A beat.)

(A beat.)

(A menacing feeling begins and builds, in sound and in light.)

(The wall opens and spits **HELEN** *back out.)*

(She looks stunned and, for the first time, her composure is badly dented. She and her clothes are soaking wet.)

(It might start to rain. Only very lightly.)

(She pulls herself together. She walks into:)

Twelve

(Their living room suddenly. **JORIS** *is pacing.* **HELEN** *sits on a couch edge, damp.)*

JORIS. – and then he said *Nyet Dos Passoso.*

So I think we need to get rid of Dos entirely.

HELEN. Did he say why?

JORIS. Moscow has concerns about his friends. His best friend, José Robles.

(A beat, he takes **HELEN** *in fully.)*

You got rained on.

HELEN. Oh. Uh. Yeah.

JORIS. You were out?

HELEN. I went for a walk.

JORIS. Without an umbrella?

HELEN. I forgot my umbrella.

What else did Karl say?

JORIS. That was it.

HELEN. Just about Dos. And his concerning choice of friends.

JORIS. Well, Karl listened to my whole report,

(we met in his room, he was getting ready for the opera)

but he seemed pleased –

HELEN. Did he say he was pleased, or he just seemed pleased?

JORIS. Have you heard that he's *not* pleased?

HELEN. No, no, I'm just –

JORIS. Have you heard anything that I haven't heard?

HELEN. No! Have *you* heard anything that *I* haven't heard?

JORIS. No!

(A beat. They study each other uneasily.)

Where were you walking to?

HELEN. I just took a walk. Around the neighborhood.

So he said No Dos Passos, and you said...

JORIS. I said, Got it! No Dos Passos.

HELEN. And then what.

JORIS. And then it was over and we left.

HELEN. Did he leave first or did you leave first?

JORIS. ...I left first, I always leave first.

You got *that* wet walking around the neighborhood?

(A beat.)

HELEN. I just think...we need to be really really really careful.

JORIS. ...We're always careful.

HELEN. More careful than usual.

JORIS. ...Careful about what? In what way, careful?

HELEN. Nevermind.

JORIS. Helen, if there's something you aren't –

HELEN. Which of us is going to tell Dos?

JORIS. I was thinking you could.

HELEN. Why me?

JORIS. He likes you more.

You like *him* more.

HELEN. All the more reason why it should be you.

JORIS. He'll take it better from you.

HELEN. What am I supposed to say?

(A beat.)

JORIS. I know there's something you aren't telling me.

HELEN. But listen to what I *am* telling you.

JORIS. ...To be careful?

HELEN. Exactly.

*(**JORIS** can't help asking:)*

JORIS. We *did* love each other, didn't we?

HELEN. Joris...

JORIS. Because I think we did, I remember that we did? At the beginning.

But I remember a lot of things just a little bit wrong

I try to remember mostly what I'm supposed to remember and

I work pretty hard to ignore the rest.

I think we were *told* to love each other but also I think we *did.*

Do you remember?

(A beat.)

HELEN. We...actually, we did really hit it off.

JORIS. *(Swamped with relief.)* Right?? I thought you were so – *bold.*

HELEN. Bold?

JORIS. You strode around like a cowboy. I thought it was incredibly brash. And hot.

HELEN. You didn't like my movies.

JORIS. No, too experimental. But it was obvious they were good.

HELEN. *(Surprised.)* You thought my movies were good?

JORIS. Yeah.

HELEN. Oh.

I didn't know that.

I thought you didn't get them.

JORIS. Well yeah no but

It's like when you pass a church and you hear a Latin mass.

I don't speak Latin, but I still get a shiver up my spine.

I know I'm in the presence of something...powerful.

But I don't *get* mass,

do you know what I mean?

*(**HELEN**'s truly moved by this.)*

HELEN. I do, actually.

JORIS. Did you think I was a total square?

HELEN. You? Ha! No.

They said: he's going to be important to us, it's your job to support him

And I should have resented you but you were so *likable*.

JORIS. So: boring.

HELEN. Not boring! You get really intense, when you're working.

You get really obsessed with the technical stuff, which I love, actually.

And if you're not working, you're like, The Guy At The Party.

People just want to be your friend and invite you to things –

which makes you much better at being invisible, in certain ways.

(There's a darker note here, both admiration and a condemnation of sorts. **JORIS** *hears it.)*

JORIS. I guess I can't tell if we turned into something

or if we were that all along, if that's what made us so useful.

The ability to – I don't know. Compartmentalize. Compromise.

(Really asking.)

Do you know what I mean?

(A beat. She does.)

HELEN. What's started to scare me lately

is this feeling that I can't remember what was the cover story and what was the real story

what's the art and what's the plan

and what's the back-up plan

Latin mass or mass-marketing –

and what's the part of me at the center, somewhere inside all that –

Do you know what I mean?

It feels like when you walk into a room and forget what you were going to do

so you just stand there and try to remember what you were looking for –

except it's not my keys or wallet, it's...

whatever core I began by trying to protect. Whoever that person was.

(Beat.)

JORIS. Something happened. Didn't it.

HELEN. ...Yes.

JORIS. Today.

HELEN. Yes.

JORIS. And it affects us?

HELEN. Maybe. Probably. Yes.

JORIS. But you can't tell me.

HELEN. You're in more danger if you know. You know how this works, J.

JORIS. Not always. You're not always in more danger by knowing, sometimes you're in less danger by knowing.

HELEN. Not this time.

(A beat.)

JORIS. Whatever it is, *you* know. So...are you in more danger, now, or less danger?

HELEN. *(Very suddenly.)* We could leave.

Pack like we're going to Spain, but then halfway to Spain we just...evaporate. Like we were never there.

JORIS. And...go where?

HELEN. I don't know, somewhere they don't really look for people.

(A real beat. He turns the idea over. So does she.)

We could, couldn't we?

Joris...

(And **JORIS** *returns to earth.)*

JORIS. There isn't really a good way to stop. For people like me.

HELEN. But...

JORIS. But maybe you could – I don't know what happened but, if you talked to Ivor, if you said that you're getting old and you want a kid –

HELEN. A kid!

JORIS. You could ask about a different kind of job. Low risk. Off the radar.

A woman could say that sort of thing, and not raise red flags.

And maybe Ivor could find you a job as a secretary, something like that.

HELEN. I don't think I can be a secretary, Joris.

JORIS. Why not?

HELEN. Because then you're just filing all the secrets – and you don't even know what you're filing. That's even worse.

(Beat.)

What are you gonna do?

JORIS. Make this movie.

HELEN. And then?

JORIS. Make the next one.

HELEN. Because you believe in the Cause?

JORIS. Because I make movies.

HELEN. And if somebody else gave you money? The French or the British or –?

JORIS. Then I'd make *their* movies.

HELEN. And if you did something else?

JORIS. *(Honest.)* I wouldn't get out of bed in the morning.

HELEN. Even when you're being told what to make?

JORIS. Even then, a little part of you still slips through –

a little part of you gets lodged in the camera lens

in what people see and how they see it –

and you still, in tiny ways, *live.*

(A beat between them. One last try:)

HELEN. And if I asked you to run away with me?

JORIS. I hope we'd both know better.

Thirteen

(**DOS** *and* **HELEN**. *Late at night.*)

(The energy is tense between them. Attraction still there, but also, a new urgency.)

DOS. My friend is missing.

HELEN. I'm sorry to hear that.

DOS. José Robles – I told you about him when we first met.

The one who was teaching at Johns Hopkins.

HELEN. *(Lying.)* I don't remember.

DOS. Well, he went to Spain some months ago.

He got a post in the revolutionary government and then he stopped writing back to me.

HELEN. I imagine it's been hard to get letters out of Madrid.

DOS. The other day, I got a letter from his wife. Who is panicking.

HELEN. He must have been pulled into the fighting.

DOS. No, he was removed from his home in the middle of the night by a group of men.

HELEN. Fascists, I imagine –?

DOS. Russians.

(A beat.)

HELEN. Why would *Russians* –?

DOS. There seem to be a number of Russians in Spain, at the moment.

I think I mentioned that before.

HELEN. I don't remember.

(A beat. **DOS** *studies her carefully.)*

DOS. If I ask you a candid question, will you give me a candid answer?

HELEN. Please don't.

(Beat.)

DOS. You knew about this.

HELEN. No, I don't know anything.

DOS. Does Joris?

HELEN. Joris doesn't know anything either.

DOS. You don't know anything, you're just making a film.

HELEN. That's right.

And on the subject of this film, I have some bad news for you.

DOS. Do you?

HELEN. Your contributions have been invaluable, Dos, but as the artistic process unfolds, it's become clear that Ernest is just a bit better suited for this – environment. With all due respect, we're going to have to let you go.

(A beat, and then **DOS** *smiles. She wants to talk about a movie right now?)*

DOS. Where's my friend?

HELEN. *(Honestly.)* I don't know where your friend is.

DOS. Can you find out?

HELEN. No.

DOS. Can you put me in contact with someone who can find out?

HELEN. You have to be joking.

DOS. Give me a name, give me a number.

HELEN. I don't think you understand –

DOS. I've tried talking to the Spanish politicians who I used to see at dinner parties, and suddenly they won't take my calls. I've called the embassy, and I'm being stonewalled. If you can –

HELEN. You're being naïve, and you have to stop.

(Beat, trying to reset them back on track.)

I'm sorry about your friend, but I can't help you.

On the subject of the movie –

DOS. Fuck the movie. This is more important than a movie.

HELEN. That's where you're wrong.

DOS. *(Startled.)* How?

HELEN. We're all expendable. Your friend is gone? In another fifty years, who'll remember him.

If I vanished tomorrow? The world would roll on. But a movie lasts. It changes the course of culture, and culture is what people do and say in order to make the history they want to have, and so in its own way a movie changes the course of history as well. What are any one of our lives against that?

DOS. *(Looking her straight in the eyes.)* But I don't think you believe that.

(A beat between them. Measuring.)

HELEN. You seem to think you know a lot about me.

DOS. You surround yourself with people who don't observe. You and Joris both.

People who are so busy being seen that they don't take the time to observe.

HELEN. And what have you observed, exactly?

DOS. I followed you. To the Plaza. Two days ago.

I saw your dinner with your companion –

HELEN. An old friend!

DOS. An old Russian friend.

HELEN. Whatever you think you're doing, it's much more dangerous than it might feel from the safety of my living room.

DOS. You looked so unhappy.

HELEN. Ex*cuse* me?

DOS. Not your face, your face always looks the way it should look, in any given situation.

But everything else about you sort of...sank to the bottom.

(A beat.)

HELEN. I don't know what you want.

DOS. I want your help. And I want to help you.

HELEN. You think *you* can help *me*?

DOS. I'm not the kind of famous Ernest is, obviously.

And I know things can get very uncomfortable for me, you don't even have to say that,

but – I'm too famous to just disappear.

There would be too many questions, if I went to Spain and vanished

or if I went to France and vanished

or if I went anywhere and vanished.

You said that if you disappeared, the world would roll on? You're right.

But if *I* disappear, the world – for five minutes – squeals to a halt. And everybody asks: *Where did he go??* And that can be a very damaging five minutes.

The sort of five minutes you don't want to risk.

So if someone wanted to leave the country and not get vanished mid-trip… I would be the right person to travel with. Because, if they were with me, they would arrive at their intended destination.

*(**HELEN** really thinks about what **DOS** is offering.)*

HELEN. Even if I wanted to help you, I just deal with the art.

Nothing about José Robles has to do with someone like me.

DOS. *Do* you want to help me?

(A beat between them. That chemistry again.)

(A real heat. They both look away.)

HELEN. I mean where would I even go.

DOS. Where do you want to go?

Scotland? The South of France. South America!

*(A beat in which **HELEN** dreams of a life, a new life.)*

(She really dreams of it. She can almost see it.)

(A window might open in the wall. The sound of gentle rain, a palm tree blowing. Shapes and shadows of palm trees. The ocean surf. They study it.)

HELEN. …And you'd take me there.

DOS. I don't mind some travel.

HELEN. And what would I do there, wherever it was?

DOS. Whatever you want.

HELEN. *(Laughing, but.)* And who would I see? And who would I know? And who would know me, if I was on the run?

DOS. Who knows you now?

(A moment.)

HELEN. Would I make movies?

DOS. Are you making them now?

HELEN. Yes. Yes, I am.

(The brief window of fantasy closes.)

DOS. Oh come on, you yourself said –

HELEN. Not the ones I want to. And not the *way* I want to. But –

Joris said this, before. That even this way, a little part of you still slips through.

And I thought: *What a strange thing to say.*

But then...

(Beat.)

I can't help you.

DOS. Helen –

HELEN. We never had this conversation.

The conversation we had is the one where I said: Thank you for all your hard work.

And you said: That's quite all right, best of luck.

DOS. *(Sadly.)* Is that what I said?

HELEN. Or you got angry. Maybe you got angry and you shouted.

DOS. I didn't get angry.

HELEN. You were very understanding, then. I'll be sure to pass that along.

DOS. I'm going to Spain with or without the movie.

HELEN. You won't find your friend there.

DOS. How do you know?

HELEN. Because there won't be any traces of him.

Those men are good at their jobs, otherwise they wouldn't have them.

If your friend is gone, he's gone.

(A beat.)

DOS. I don't believe that we're all expendable. And I don't care about art. Art is a luxury.

I care about the way we treat each other. Who we love and what happens to them.

That's what I care about.

*(**DOS** walks offstage.)*

*(A light on **ERNEST**, in his sound booth.)*

(He's pretty drunk. Late-night. Softened up.)

(He taps the mic. Experimentally:)

ERNEST. **Spain... land of mystery.**

Tierra...incognita!

*(He looks at **HELEN**.)*

HELEN. No regrets?

ERNEST. On the contrary. I'm full of them.

Have a drink?

HELEN. You know, there are moments in which I think we understand each other.

ERNEST. I thought you didn't like me.

HELEN. No, but I don't like myself that much either.

ERNEST. Oh, well, same.

(A moment between them that is a softening.)

Did you read my screenplay?

HELEN. I did.

ERNEST. And?

HELEN. It's really good.

(This is a gift, and **ERNEST** *receives it.)*

(He gives her one back:)

ERNEST. If it helps at all, once we get to the war, you won't even have time to think.

You'll just be in it, the thing that's happening all around you. You won't even exist.

HELEN. That was why I liked making movies.

ERNEST. *(Winningly.)* Two-for-one.

HELEN. Does it get better?

ERNEST. Not really.

HELEN. I didn't even tell you which "it" I meant.

ERNEST. The answer stands.

(Shared gallows humor.)

HELEN. You know, I think I will take that drink after all.

*(***ERNEST** *hands her one.)*

*(***JORIS** *walks onstage. Suitcase in hand.)*

JORIS. Time for Spain!

ERNEST. To Spain!

HELEN. *(Lifts her drink.)* To Spain.

(And the whole world shifts.)

Fourteen
The War

(An opera, about The Great Single-Sentence War.)

(This is both a fantasia, and a piece of propaganda.)

(Here is one way this could go:)

(A thick haze of smoke.)

(A glorious shaft of light cuts through it.)

(A wheelbarrow appears. An olive tree. Rolling fog.)

*(***KARL*** in the midst of it.* **KARL** *the Noble Peasant is called to defend his country.)*

*(***HELEN***,* **JORIS** *and* **DOS** *cross into the War Opera.)*

(All of our characters meet – briefly – in this no-man's-land of beautiful lies. They take **KARL** *in as they pass him and vanish into the mist.)*

*(***KARL*** sings. Operatically. Beautifully. His voice swallows the whole room.)*

KARL.

LA TIERRA ESTÁ SECA	*THIS EARTH IS DRY*
AL NORTE NOS VAMOS	*TO THE NORTH WE GO*
TUVIMOS LA TIERRA	*WE HAD THE EARTH*
AL SOL LA QUEMAMOS	*WE BURNED IT IN THE SUN*
REZAMOS POR LA LLUVIA	*WE PRAY FOR RAIN*
SOÑAMOS CON LA GUERRA	*WE DREAM ABOUT THE WAR*

ESPAÑA ES NUESTRA	*SPAIN IS OURS*
DEBEMOS SALVAR-LA	*WE MUST SAVE IT*
EL CAMINO ESTÁ LIBRE	*THE ROAD IS FREE*
SEIS DEVIENEN CINCO	*SIX MEN BECOME FIVE*
Y CUATRO SON TRES	*THEN FOUR ARE THREE*
LOS TRES QUE SE QUEDAN	*THE THREE THAT STAYED*
REZAMOS POR LA LLUVIA	*WE PRAY FOR RAIN*
LUCHAMOS POR ESPAÑA	*WE FIGHT FOR SPAIN*
EL PUENTE ES NUESTRO	*THE BRIDGE IS OURS*
EL CAMINO SE SALVA	*THE ROAD IS SAVED*

(Across the song, a moment of magic or sleight-of-hand: maybe his shovel becomes a gun. Or he picks up a tree branch and it becomes a gun. Or the barren tree behind him explodes into blossoms. Or water flows suddenly where there was dry earth. Etc.)

*(***KARL***'s operatic song builds and builds and builds until –)*

(An explosion! A bullet finds his noble chest.)

(Blackout as **KARL** *stumbles backward, and:)*

(A spotlight appears, on **HELEN**. *In the midst of the fog and rubble, whatever is left of the War Opera. Her voice is close and intimate, the way* **ERNEST***'s was in his recording booth. She may or may not speak into a visible mic in the same way he did, but her voice should be mic'd.)*

HELEN. A few nights before we left for Spain, Ivor asked to see me at his hotel.

It was raining lightly.

I took a cab part of the way, and then I walked part of the way.

I had an umbrella with me, and the rain fell very steady and straight and I didn't get wet.

We ate dinner in the restaurant, publicly, like old friends – hidden in plain sight.

But afterward, Ivor invited me up to his room, which was unusual.

After he dismissed his bodyguards, he brought me into the bathroom, and he turned on the shower and with all his clothes on, he stepped under the spray.

And he gestured for me to join him.

So I did.

And with the water thundering down on us,

he put his mouth very close to my ear

and he told me a number of things.

Moscow had started the Purges, he said, just the week before.

High level generals and strategists and commanders – rounded up, tortured.

The accusation was that they were spies.

I said to Ivor, "That doesn't make sense. Why is Stalin doing this?"

And Ivor said: *These men had become powerful.*

I asked Ivor why he was telling me.

There can be a lot of – well, let's call it turnover – in this line of work,

a lot of He-said-He-said, and it's so rarely my business.

And Ivor said: *It's bad right now and it's gonna get a lot worse.*

My advice is, hit the floor and stay flat until it's over.

I said: "I'm just a filmmaker, I'm just a filmmaker's *girlfriend*. How are we in danger?"

And he said: *Because films are powerful and so are the people who make them.*

Why, did you think you and Joris were just doing this for fun?

And I – it's funny because I've said so much

about the power and value of what we do

and sometimes I believe it and sometimes I don't

but I've never, myself, felt powerful.

Not until I realized I had become killable.

Because of the thing we were making

Joris and I had become...killable.

(A moment, really thinking about this.)

(The wonder of it, the strangeness.)

(The compliment of it. The fear.)

And then I went home.

And we went to Spain.

And it was chaos.

We shot footage of rolling fields and rubble

and footage of the boys Ernest described:

good-looking and tired and nobly wounded.

And yes, many of them were hit

by the ricochet from their own guns;

and yes, we shot rubble from three different angles

to look like three different towns;

and yes, the whole time, I waited for a bullet to find the back of my head,

or men in the night to kick down my door –

any men, could have been any men –

But we built a single beautiful sentence out of a muddy howl.

And the way it felt – to take all of that mess and turn it into...

a kind of salvation...

I could have left Joris, I could have left my name.

But being an *artist*. Even like this. Even like this.

How could I leave that behind.

(A beat.)

And yet late at night, every night, I find myself asking:

Can a false story be so good that it does something true?

Or are we just telling lies that will travel down the decades

until we're in a future built on those lies?

And what does that future look like?

(A beat.)

(And the whole world shifts again.)

Fifteen

(A conference room is revealed.)

(Contemporary: stripped, efficient. Bleak.)

(We've jumped in time to the present, but everybody looks the same. Time is a blink. Time means nothing, because history is just an endless loop.)

*(***JORIS***,* ***HELEN*** *and* ***ERNEST*** *sit at the conference table.* ***DOS*** *as well, a little apart from them. He isn't thrilled to be here. Everybody is wearing their previous clothes, though maybe with a lanyard or a tech-y Patagonia vest over the top.* ***KARL*** *stands at the head, and addresses them.* ***KARL*** *has a Russian accent, but he now speaks in easy casual English.)*

KARL. Look, you've all done such a great job, and I just want to congratulate you on the whole Spanish thing. So, congrats! A round of applause.

(He claps.)

*(***ERNEST*** *and* ***JORIS*** *both clap as well, uncertainly.)*

*(***HELEN*** *and* ***DOS*** *don't.)*

OK!

Your next job – lean in guys, this is exciting – your next job is: the internet.

DOS. The...next job?

KARL. Yes! Movies are – passé. Declassé. Movies aren't the thing anymore.

HELEN. They're not?

KARL. No, now the thing is the internet. A few of our guys are gonna come in and show you the general lay of the land in terms of social media –

HELEN. I...feel weird about the internet.

KARL. "Weird about the internet"...

JORIS. I mean we can learn how to – that's fine, we'll learn how to –

HELEN. Maybe there's some *other* – maybe we could make a series of really moving books, or books on *tape* –

KARL. No no no

Times have changed, things have changed.

You can't just *make art* if you want to effect change.

DOS. I thought that was the whole thing. Art as –

ERNEST. *(Helpfully.)* – radical brain surgery.

KARL. Art as *brain* surgery?? Eugh, no thank you.

ERNEST. I just mean –

DOS. You know, I think I'm good, so I'm just gonna –

(He starts to stand.)

KARL. *(Polite but forcefully.)* Sit down please.

*(**DOS** hesitates, then sits.)*

Would anybody like some bottled water? I'm gonna grab some bottled water, would anybody –?

HELEN, DOS & JORIS. No thank you / no thanks / I'm OK.

ERNEST. I'll take some.

KARL. Okay! OK. Bottled water! Coming right up.

(He goes to the wall, opens a door, leans in.)

(**KARL** *returns with bottled waters, which he distributes to all of them.)*

KARL. OK where were we. The future! The internet is the future.

HELEN. I'm so sorry, I'm not trying to be difficult at all

I just – can you just help me understand –

what you meant when you said, just a minute ago –

about movies being *passé*?

KARL. Sure! Movies. Who watches them?

HELEN. I mean – everyone.

JORIS. A lot of people.

KARL. Okay. Okay, sure: "A lot of people watch a lot of movies." Would you say that's a fair statement?

HELEN. I mean...yes?

KARL. "A lot of people watch a lot of movies, and a lot of movies are available to be watched." Yes?

JORIS. Yeah! That's true, right?

ERNEST. *(Cheerful.)* So many movies! How're you supposed to have time to watch them all.

KARL. That is *right.*

That is exactly *right*!

How *are* you supposed to have time to watch them all?

You don't! People don't. And there you go, that's the problem.

HELEN. *(Timidly.)* But – that's a good thing? That movies are in demand?

KARL. Ah. I see. I see the fallacy under which you're laboring.

(Let me clarify this for you:)

Movies are discardable. Movies are: you wipe your nose and you throw it away.

Movies are: put one on and shove popcorn in your walrus face.

Do you see what I mean now?

Everybody can find anything they want to watch.

"Radical brain surgery" doesn't work when you're presented with a buffet.

"Radical brain surgery" works when everyone around you is receiving *one* set of ideas. Convincingly. Seductively. You're discussing it, you're going home and thinking about it, you're rewiring your friends and neighbors as you get rewired. Bam! You've changed a generation.

But no one movie will do that any longer.

Do you see now?

JORIS. But...we could make a – really provocative –

We could *make* everybody look.

KARL. Could you? Maybe. But they don't wanna look. They're tired and they're watching Netflix and they're watching the news and they're too tired to watch the things they're watching so they're scrolling on their phones at the same time and, you know, maybe they even have the volume turned low, maybe you're on mute.

So much for your new movie.

HELEN. So...what are you saying?

KARL. Art is dead.

Your new job is the internet.

(A beat.)

JORIS. *(Weakly.)* I was wondering if maybe Hel and I could – go on a brief vacation?

KARL. Vacation?!

HELEN. It's OK, it's not important.

*(**DOS** looks at her with compassion.)*

(She can't meet his eyes.)

KARL. I think you think this job is gonna be hard, Joris, but it's not gonna be hard.

You just make a bunch of different characters – just think of them as characters! – and they're on different platforms. But they're all saying the same thing. It's like a special kind of movie basically, for a special kind of audience. All new! But not so different. Not so hard.

ERNEST. *(Quietly but very sincerely.)* The death of art feels hard.

KARL. Sure, sure. I mean, sure, we all felt that for a while.

But it's good to know how things work, that's always exhilarating, frankly, to be ahead of the game.

You guys look so glum! Trust me, this is good!

HELEN. *(Genuinely asking.)* But you like opera?

KARL. Excuse me?

HELEN. I heard that – It's come up, that you really like opera?

KARL. Yeah, I love it! It's my favorite thing.

HELEN. So if you like opera...

I mean – literally nobody goes to the opera. But you still – you still find it valuable?

KARL. I see. I see what you're asking.

I find it personally valuable, yes.

Opera is meaningless as a mode of controlling thought, shifting global power dynamics and impacting governance. But to me, personally, it's very valuable.

HELEN. But if you're *personally* moved by it

if you're *personally* shifted

and you are a *person* who is controlling modes of thought and – all that other stuff, Changing The World – then...

isn't opera also changing the world?

(A beat.)

KARL. You want to make an opera?

HELEN. No, I hate opera. Personally.

KARL. You want to make an argument for opera as a tool for, say, determining elections?

HELEN. No.

KARL. Then what?

HELEN. I guess I'm just asking...

Aside from the job, aside from the new mechanics of the next job, I'm just asking...

(This comes from the heart.)

Don't you still believe in art?

(A real beat.)

*(**ERNEST** and **DOS** and **JORIS** lean in for the answer.)*

KARL. *(Definitively.)* No.

(A beat.)

HELEN. Oh.

(A beat.)

KARL. *(To them all, cheerful.)* Any other questions?

(They're sort of emotionally destroyed.)

(They glance at each other, glance at the floor.)

JORIS, DOS, ERNEST & HELEN. No / no / I don't think so / not really

KARL. Okay great! Training starts tomorrow in the big computer lab downstairs, nine a.m., don't forget your key cards, bring two forms of ID. Everybody have a great night!

(They get up. In disarray. Bewildered and a little broken.)

*(***ERNEST*** gathers all the unopened water bottles and takes them with him.)*

*(***ERNEST, DOS, JORIS*** and ***HELEN*** file out.)*

*(***KARL*** is left alone.)*

(He straightens up the conference room table.)

(He starts to hum a line of melody from an opera. He hums louder as he straightens.)

(He breaks into song and sings. His voice is gorgeous and pure and the moment is absolutely beautiful. Simple and soaring and human.)

(Almost as if it means something.)

(Almost as if he were wrong.)

(Almost as if all that we make will outlive us, and the life it continues to have in our absence will still have meaning.)

(Almost.)

(Lights down.)

End of Play

APPENDIX

Below is a Russian translation of **KARL**'s speech on page 68. This text was translated by Tatyana Khaikin for the Second Stage production.

ДОС ПАСОС и есть проблема.

ДОС ПАСОС слишком много думает

ДОС ПАСОС говорит по-испански

ДОС ПАСОС ест слишком много овощей

ДОС ПАСОС пьет умеренно,

а человеку, который умеренно пьет, нельзя доверять – как ДОС ПАСОСУ!

Прощай, ДОС ПАСОС

Избавиться от ДОС ПАСОСА

Нет ДОС ПАСОСУ!

Dos Passos i yest' prablema.

Dos Passos slishkum mnoga dumaet

Dos Passos gavarit po ispanski

Dos Passos yest slishkum mnoga ovoshei

Dos Passos umereno p'yot

A cheloveku katoryi umereno p'yot nil'zya daveryat' – kak Dos Passosu!

Prashchai Dos Passos

Izbavit'sya ot Dos Passosa

Net Dos Passosu!

www.ingramcontent.com/pod-product-compliance
Lightning Source LLC
Jackson TN
JSHW011950131224
75386JS00042B/1657

9780573711107